P9-DGJ-826

Heryin Books
1033 E. Main St., #202, Alhambra, CA 91801
Printed in Taiwan
www.heryin.com

Library of Congress Cataloging-in-Publication Data
Chen, Zhiyuan, 1975-
The featherless chicken / written & illustrated by Chih-Yuan Chen.
-- 1st English ed.p. cm.
Summary: Scorned at first by others, a featherless chicken
finds a way to fit in before discovering that his new friends
may not be as beautiful as they appear to be.
[1. Chickens--Fiction. 2. Beauty, Personal--Fiction. 3.
Self-acceptance--Fiction.] I. Title.
PZ7.C41817Fea 2006 [E]--dc22 2006000813
ISBN-13 : 978-0-9762-0569-2
ISBN-10 : 0-9762-0569-6

The Featherless Chicken

Chih-Yuan Chen

Heryin Books
Alhambra, California

In a beautiful patch of flowers,
an egg lay, waiting.

One day, the egg jiggled
and cracked and wiggled
and snapped, until a thin
little chicken burst out of
the shell without a single
feather on his body. He was
a featherless chicken.

When the wind blew,
the featherless chicken
would catch cold.

His sensitive nose
was also allergic to
pollen. He sneezed
and sneezed.

One day, the lonely little chicken saw four other chickens walking out of the forest. They were the most beautiful chickens he'd ever seen. They had feathers. Splendid feathers! They strutted along with their heads held high. The featherless chicken was curious. "Where are you going?" Without even turning their heads, the four replied, "Boating!"

"Oh, could I come too?"
Now the four beautiful chickens looked him over,
from naked top to naked toe.
"Oh no. We don't play with chickens without
feathers." Then they tipped their beaks up high
and stepped into their boat.

The featherless chicken was sad.
His eyes filled with tears.

He tripped on a stone, and fell into
a puddle. His body was covered with sticky
mud, and an old soup can sat on his head.

A strong wind began to blow,
and like an artist, the wind decorated the chicken's muddy body with leaves and papers, and other random things.
For the first time in his life,
the chicken didn't feel cold. The leaves fluttered like feathers. He looked down at himself. He was beautiful!

15
15
19

The four chickens in the boat noticed the featherless chicken's new look. "Ooh," they squawked. "I've never seen such a gorgeous chicken! And that hat is simply the tops!" They rowed back to shore to invite the featherless chicken to join them on their outing.

In the boat, the five chickens had a lively debate over who was the most beautiful. To call attention to themselves, they all began flapping their wings. It was too much for the featherless chicken's sensitive nose. He let loose an explosive sneeze.

The boat rocked wildly.
All five chickens squished
and squawked and ran around
in terror, and the boat
started to tip ...

With a whoosh and a whack,
the boat flipped.
All the chickens splashed
into the lake.

As the water of the lake finally grew still,
things started to appear.
One of them was the featherless chicken,
spluttering for breath. The leaves
that had covered his body were completely
washed away. "Oh no!" he cried.

134
140

Then, the other chickens popped up...
one... two... three... four.
Four featherless chickens!

Everyone stared in horror at each other's bare bodies. They shook their heads in disbelief.

He couldn't help it. The featherless chicken started to laugh, and one by one, all the chickens joined him, chortling and cackling until they gasped for breath.

On shore, the five chickens
shook the water off their slick backs.
"Hey," said the featherless chicken.
"That was fun. Let's go again tomorrow!"
The others paused and thought for a moment,
then replied: "Great idea!"

And with that, the five featherless chickens
strutted off to the forest together.